D0766024

A L I S
1880486

For Jason, the helmsman

www.dragonbloodpirates.co.uk

ORCHARD BOOKS
338 Euston Road, London NW1 3BH

First published in 2008 by Lothian Children's Books,
an imprint of Hachette Livre Australia
First published in the UK in 2010 by Orchard Books

ISBN 978 1 40830 741 0

A CIP catalogue record for this book is available from the British Library.

10 9 8 7 6 5 4 3 2 1

Printed in Great Britain by J F Print Ltd., Sparkford
Orchard Books is a division of Hachette Children's Books,
an Hachette UK company.

www.hachette.co.uk

Jewels of the Jolly Roger

Dan Jerris

N
W
E
S
Death Islan
Shipwreck Island.
Cannibal Island

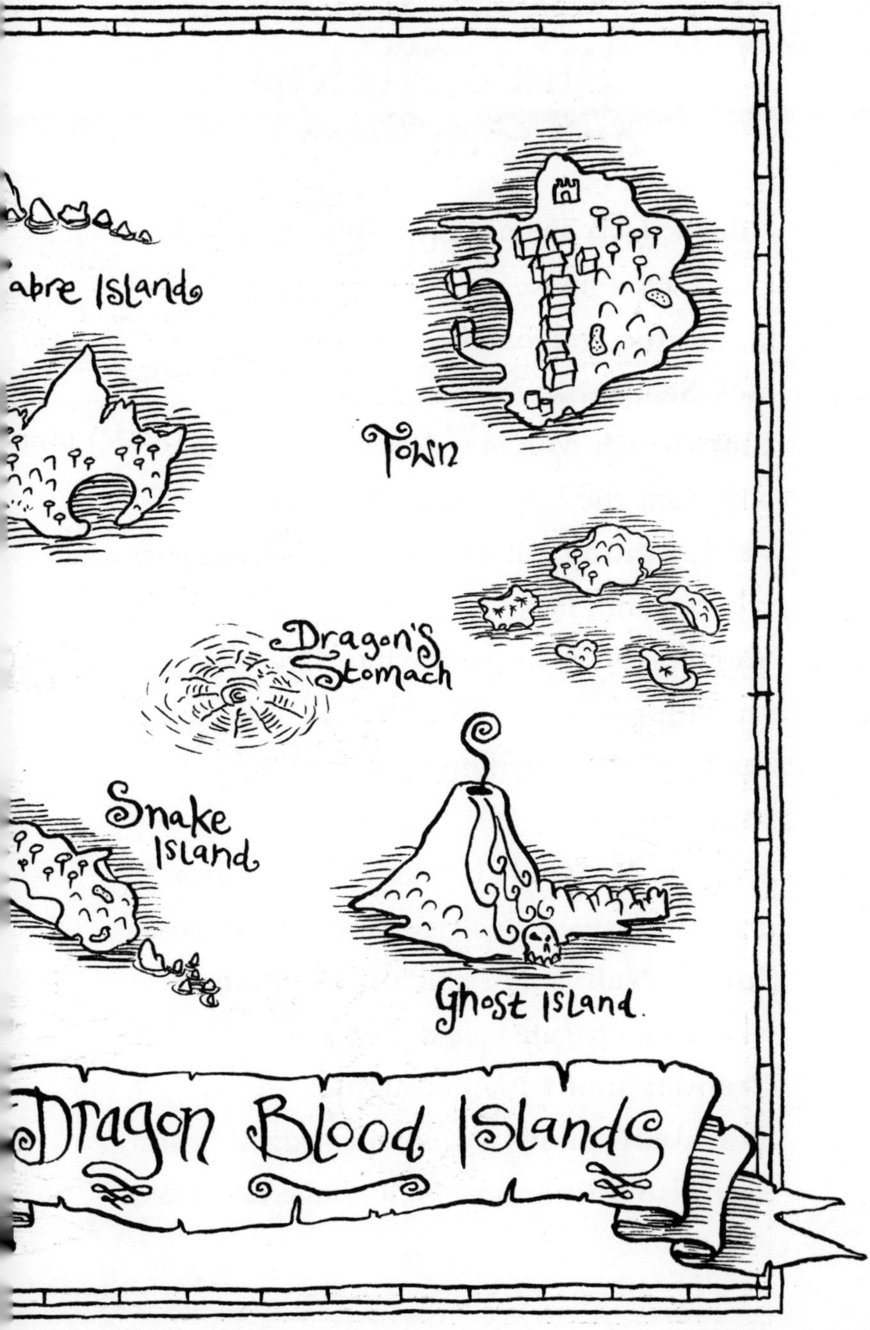

abre Island

Town

Dragon's Stomach

Snake Island

Ghost Island.

Dragon Blood Islands

Pirate Mateys and Scallywags

Alleric (Al) Breas: Lives in Drake Drive and owns a mysterious sea trunk that takes him to the Dragon Blood Islands.

Jack Seabrook: Al's best friend.

Blacktooth McGee: A very nasty pirate who runs the brigantine *The Revenge.*

Flash Johnny: Blacktooth's devious and greedy cabin boy.

Snakeboot: A magical white three-legged cat with purple eyes. Legend has it he once belonged to a terrifying pirate called Vicious Victor.

Pigface McNurt: Blacktooth's bosun; a massive pirate with a ring through his nose.

Snotty Nell: A horrible one-eyed pirate who sails a frigate called *The Tormentor.*

Grenda: Snotty Nell's daughter.

Sharkbait: Snotty Nell's one-legged bosun.

Vampire Zu: Snotty Nell's huge first mate.

Gunner: The pirate captain of the ship *The Booty.*

Mozzy: *The Booty*'s bosun (petty officer).

Slicer: *The Booty*'s cook.

Mahoot: Captain Gunner's cabin boy.

Grandfather: Mahoot's grandfather and guardian of the swimming elephants on Sabre Island.

Stanley Spong: A crooked, sneaky trader who cheats people.

Vicious Victor: A pirate ghost. He used to pillage the Dragon Blood Islands and he stole Prince Alleric's magical sabre.

Prince Alleric: The prince who once ruled Sabre Island but disappeared in mysterious circumstances.

Halimeda (Hally) Breas: Al's younger sister.

Greeny Joe: A shark so big and old that mould grows on his skin, making him glow green in the dark.

Sabre Island

Snakeboot, the three-legged white cat, sat purring happily on an old sea trunk in the attic of Alleric Breas's house at number five Drake Drive. Al and his best friend, Jack, were also in the attic.

"Hally's playing next door," said Al. "It might be a good time to go back to Sabre Island."

"I know it sounds mean, but it would be good to go back on our own," said

Jack. "Captain Gunner's ship, *The Booty*, might still be there. And I really want to go hunting for treasure!"

"It's not really being mean," said Al. "Hally didn't want to go to sea again, anyway. She said she was too scared to go to Cannibal Island. I don't think she'll mind if we go on our own."

"Do you think we could get back to exactly the same time and place as when we left?" Jack asked his friend.

Snakeboot arched his back, jumped down from the sea trunk and clawed at the lock on the front of the trunk.

"I think Snakeboot is saying yes," Al replied. "And I can't wait to see if that treasure map we found in Alleric Castle really leads us to jewels and gold."

"Let's get dressed, then." Jack reached up and pulled down two sets of pirate clothes from a shelf.

The boys quickly changed clothes. Al grabbed an old iron key and unlocked the sea trunk. He lifted the lid and Snakeboot leapt inside. The boys stepped into the trunk and, with a bright flash of light, they faded and disappeared.

Seconds later they reappeared in an abandoned gazebo in the jungle, precisely the place they had disappeared from only days before. In front of them, lying on the floor, were four empty buckets, just as they had left them. They picked up the buckets and made their way to a bubbling creek.

Captain Gunner, looking very smart in his black frockcoat and tricorn hat, approached them. "Hurry up!" he yelled. "You two are slacking off. Mahoot has made four trips while you've been lazing around. We're nearly ready to set sail for Cannibal Island."

Al and Jack smiled at each other. No one had missed them. "Sorry, Captain Gunner," said Al, "but we just had to say goodbye to Hally. She's happy not to be coming with us this time."

A boy about Al and Jack's age appeared along the track, carrying two full buckets of water. "Hello, you two." He smiled.

"Sorry, Mahoot, we got sidetracked," said Jack, "but we're back on duty now."

"These buckets are heavy," replied Mahoot. "I'll keep going and see you on *The Booty*."

"If young Hally's not coming with us you'd better get those barrels filled with water," Captain Gunner said. "The tide's in at four this afternoon, and we don't want to miss it." He turned and marched off down the track towards his ship.

"We did it!" whispered Jack, as he bent over the creek and filled his buckets. "We're getting better and better at coming and going from the Dragon Blood Islands."

The boys carried their buckets down the track to *The Booty*'s lifeboat, trying not to spill too much on the way.

"Lazy blighters," said Slicer, the cook, as Al and Jack emptied their buckets into

the barrel set in the lifeboat. He turned to Mahoot. "You've filled two barrels and worked hard so *you* can go back to *The Booty*." Slicer looked long and hard at Al and Jack. "You two have been slow and lazy, so you'll do double duty till the

rest of the barrels are filled."

"Let's get it over with," said Al as he turned and trudged back up the track to the creek. "It will be worth all the hard work if we find the treasure on that map from Alleric Castle."

Sneaking Past the Jolly Roger

In the dead of night, with a following breeze, Captain Gunner stood on the poop deck of *The Booty*. "There are only two places that give safe anchorage on Cannibal Island," he explained to Al, Jack and Mahoot, as they studied the treasure map. "This map shows the second anchorage. Annoyingly, it's further around, past Blacktooth's fort, which means we'll have to sail right past the blasted thing. To top it off, the landing beach is right near the cannibals' camp."

"Can we approach from another direction, rather than go near Blacktooth?" asked Al.

"No," replied the captain. "There's a reef that runs along the island and Blacktooth guards the only entrance. We're gunner have to try to sneak past him. Mozzy!" he called to his bosun standing at the helm. "I want you to hoist the black sails. I don't want any reflection from the moonlight." Captain Gunner lifted his voice so it boomed across the ship. "I want total silence from here on or I'm gunner kill the first man who even sneezes!"

"Aye, aye," the crew responded.

With black sails billowing, *The Booty* had to make a tack under the walls of a large wooden fort. At anchor, just in front of the fort, was Blacktooth's ship, *The Revenge*.

"They're home, unfortunately," whispered Mahoot, as he and the rest of the crew peered intently at the forbidding walls nearby. On a large lookout tower, the Jolly Roger, the black flag with the white grinning skull and crossbones, fluttered. The skull glowed in the moonlight. Slicer clutched his sword nervously as *The Booty* almost touched the shore below the fort. The bosun tightened a loose halyard so it didn't rattle against the mast in the breeze.

The Booty slid silently past and the fort disappeared behind them. Mahoot let out a huge sigh of relief. "Made it," he said under his breath.

They sailed on with a rocky reef on one side and a white chalk cliff on the shore. Pounding waves crashed over the reef and a huge rip tide dragged the ship sideways. With the surging currents and the white foam making the entrance extremely treacherous, only Captain Gunner's seamanship saved them from being shipwrecked. The pirates cheered once they were through and on their way to begin their treasure hunt.

They may not have cheered quite so loudly if they had realised there was a sharp-eyed lookout standing just under the Jolly Roger on the fort. "Sail! Sail! Sail at two o'clock!" the lookout cried. A large, brutish pirate with a fat face and a ring through his nose ran up to the top of the tower. "See, Pigface?" the lookout said, pointing. "That's a sail. It's passing between the reef and the cliffs and it's heading for Cannibal Bay."

Pigface McNurt, Captain Blacktooth's first mate, stared at the dark ship highlighted against the white cliffs and the surf. "It's a carrack," he said, squinting into the darkness. "There's only one carrack I know of in these parts – *The Booty.* What could she want here? If they go ashore, the cannibals will eat them the minute they land. And they're using black sails. Maybe that stupid pirate plans to sneak up from

Cannibal Bay and attack us. I'd better go and warn the captain."

When Blacktooth found out what was happening, he scowled. "I've had it with that sscoundrel Gunner and his sscab-faced crew," he said. "We'll go after them and attack firsst. Pigface, call the crew to armss!"

Shrunken Heads

At first light Captain Gunner ordered the lowering of the longboat. Snakeboot was the first to jump to the sand, then the crew of *The Booty* followed. They pulled the longboat up onto the beach and hid it under some branches. “We don’t want the cannibals finding it and searching for us,” explained Slicer.

Gunner and his pirate crew headed down the beach towards a bluff. “The first marker should be a Jolly Roger and we should find it near the headland," said Gunner, holding the map out as he walked. "Everyone look for some sort of mark so we can start our search."

The pirates fanned out at his command and hunted high and low in the scrub at the end of the beach.

"If I were leaving a clue to the treasure," said Al, "I'd choose a place that wouldn't blow away or get chopped down or knocked

over. I reckon we should look at the base of the cliff."

"Good idea," said Jack. The boys rock-hopped to the base of the cliff and scanned the rocks and overhangs for a drawing or mark.

"Look," said Mahoot, pointing, "there's a skull and crossbones carved in that rock."

"Let's get Captain Gunner!" said Al.

Minutes later, the pirates began their hunt. "A hundred paces," called Captain

Gunner, "and we should find another mark. Then there are some trees with heads drawn on them. I wonder what that means?"

One hundred paces later the search for a sign began again, but this time Jack found a Jolly Roger carved on a flat rock, almost overgrown with moss.

"We go right," said Gunner. "And I warn you all, keep your eyes open and your mouths shut. We're entering cannibal territory and we don't want any noise to attract them. We have to find these odd trees, then we have to get to the middle of the island on our own, as there are no more clues on the map."

The pirates crept through a trail in the jungle. Gunner, who was leading, accidentally knocked a wasps' nest hanging from a branch. The wasps buzzed in fury. Mozzy gave out a loud yell as he was stung. The other pirates leapt and jumped, but clamped their hands over their mouths so they couldn't cry out, and ran for all they were worth.

Al, Jack and Mahoot turned and ran back down the trail. They waited till the wasps stopped buzzing, then crept back up the path, avoiding the nest.

The crew groaned in pain. Captain Gunner's nose was twice its normal size. Mozzy had one eye closed. Slicer's lips were swollen and the rest of the pirates didn't look any better.

As they had no medicine to fix the stinging pain, the pirates screwed up their faces in misery and continued on their journey.

Soon the path became wider and the pirates were able to quicken their pace. Al was looking upwards every now and then, in case someone else brushed a wasps' nest, when he noticed something in a tree just above Gunner's hat. He stopped as his eyes widened in horror.

The hideous shrunken head of a dead man stared back at him. The skin on the disembodied face was wrinkled and blackened. Two shrivelled eyes still held a look of fear. The gruesome sight took away Al's power of speech, so he grabbed Jack's shoulder in a vice-like grip.

His friend stopped. Al pointed up and Jack's mouth dropped open in shock. Jack grabbed Mahoot. Mahoot looked up. He took to his heels and grabbed Captain Gunner. Then all the pirates looked up. Surrounding them, shrunken heads, with agonised expressions frozen on their features, stared down at the intruders.

"They must have died horrible deaths," whispered Slicer.

Al shuddered.

The fearful pirates now walked very

slowly, clutching their sabres, their nerves making them jump at every sound. They hadn't gone far when an ominous moan shivered their blood. Just to one side, a shrunken head moved. Opening its mouth, it wailed in a ghostly voice, "I once sailed under the Jolly Roger. I am damned!"

Another head beside Captain Gunner cried, "Run, run, before the cannibals eat you and shrink your head over a fire!"

Al's heart leapt into his throat.

Suddenly all the ghoulish heads began to moan. Captain Gunner broke out in a cold sweat which dripped from his swollen nose. "They're haunted!" he shrieked.

"Dinner you'll be!" howled another ghastly head. "Turn back, run!"

Mozzy fell to his knees. "Don't kill us!" he gibbered in fear.

In answer, the horrible heads began to

sing. Their spine-chilling words shattered the nerves of the pirates:

"Ooey gooey custard and green maggot pie,
Two pirates' livers and one cat's eye.
If the Jolly Roger is what you fly,
Then you will be the next to die.
The cannibals'll put you in a pot, add heat
Then boil you up and eat, eat, eat!"

Quicksand

Panicked, the pirates, with their grown-up legs, thundered off and left the boys behind. Jack, Mahoot and Al sprinted after them. Terrified, they came out of the jungle into a mossy glade, just in time to see their friends sinking in front of their eyes. "Help! Help!" came the cries of the sinking pirates, frantically waving their arms and struggling against the sucking mud. The more they tried to escape, the faster they were sucked downwards into the ground. "Quicksand!" moaned Captain Gunner fearfully. "We're doomed!"

"Quicksand?" Jack asked, looking in bewilderment at the sinking pirates in front of him.

"It's sticky mud," Al explained. "I've read about it." He called out to the pirates, "Stop struggling! The more you struggle the faster

you'll sink. We'll save you. Just keep still."

The pirates stopped squealing and wriggling and waited with their eyes popping out in terror to see what the boys could do.

Al held out his hand to Mozzy, who was nearest to him. "Toss us your sword," he called to the pirate. Mozzy unbuckled his belt and threw his sword to Al.

Al took the sword and cut a strong branch from a nearby tree. Then the boys lay on the ground and held the branch out to Mozzy. When he grabbed the branch the boys pulled him from the squelching mud. Once Mozzy was free, he cut another branch, and they freed two more pirates. In a very short time the pirate crew were safe. They sat beside the quicksand desperately trying to catch their breath.

Gunner rallied his crew. He held the map out for all to see. "We've come this far," he told his men. "We're not giving in.

There's treasure to be found and the map says it's somewhere here in the middle of the island. We're gunner press on and we're gunner be the ones to find it. We don't want Blacktooth to get it, do we?"

His words were interrupted by a hair-raising shout coming from the jungle behind them. The ghostly voices of the shrunken heads had begun singing again. Over the eerie hum of their song, came human wails of dread.

"Who could that be?" Gunner asked, looking around in disbelief.

In answer, a loud and instantly recognisable voice carried to them. "Ssstop being sssilly ssissiess. Gunnerss's crew hass come through here, I can ssee their big boot printss. If they made it, sso can we."

"It's Blacktooth," exclaimed Al.

"Quick," hissed Gunner, "we don't want him to find us."

"Which way?" asked Al.

"Away from the treasure, so back towards the coast. Just follow me," ordered Gunner. The pirate crew quickly made their way back towards *The Booty*, and away from the quicksand, the horrible wailing heads and Blacktooth.

The only way was through the jungle, but the trees and vines were so thick that each of them had to hack his way past, so they made slow progress. Eventually, when everyone was exhausted, Gunner called them to a halt. "We're gunner get lost," he puffed. "Only one person needs to hack at a time if we form a line. Everyone, hang onto the man's belt in front of you."

They set off again and Captain Gunner used his sword to cut a path. Eventually, the vines cleared and the pirates made their way out onto a beach. At anchor in the bay were two ships, *The Booty* and *The Revenge*.

"We can only hope Blacktooth's been swallowed by the quicksand and isn't still after us," said Slicer, looking at their enemy's ship.

Gunner looked around at his dejected men. Al was looking around too. Something was missing. "Snakeboot!" he called.

"I haven't seen him for ages," said Jack. "It all became so crazy, I didn't look out for him."

"That cat has nine lives at least," said Captain Gunner. "We won't leave him on the island, don't worry. Let's press on and find that treasure. What do you think, men?"

The pirates, exhausted as they were, raised their fists. "Aye, Captain, that we will!" they cried.

Gunner smiled. "And Snakeboot will find us when we least expect it," he reassured the boys. "So, we're gunner look for the cat and the treasure and this time we'll be behind Blacktooth." With those words he turned and set off down the path.

Cannibals

Captain Gunner's crew started their treasure hunt once again, and this time they took great care to watch their every step. With all the heat and excitement they were worn out and very thirsty. Luckily, just as they got back to the Shrunken Head Jungle, Al and Jack heard the faint bubbling of a small stream. The boys quickly tapped Slicer on the back.

"Slicer, a stream," whispered Al.

"We could all have a drink." Slicer tapped the man in front of him and this continued until all the pirates had turned around to follow Al towards the inviting water. But he had only taken a few steps when he stumbled. Down at his feet was an almost invisible cord, hidden in the earth. Al grabbed it and, hand over hand, he and the crew followed it through the bushes.

Soon Al arrived at a tree with a shrunken head attached. He pulled the cord. The head moved and the mouth opened. Al reached up and tapped it and it fell to the ground with an odd plop. Al picked it up and shook it. It felt odd so he broke a piece off. "It's made of rubber!" he cried.

The pirates looked at each other in puzzlement. "What's rubber?" they asked.

"It's a man-made material," explained Al. "It comes from the sap of a tree."

"Never heard of it," said Gunner.

"Never mind," said Jack. "How about we follow the cord back and see who's pulling the strings around here?"

The pirates sneaked back through the jungle, following the cord. It wasn't long before they came to a large hollow tree. Captain Gunner leapt to the entrance and waved his sword.

A screech of fear came from the person hiding inside. But instead of attacking, Captain Gunner put his sword in its scabbard, bent down and said, "There,

there, we won't hurt you."

The boys crept up and there, quaking in terror as she gazed upon the dirty, monstrous swollen faces of the pirates surrounding her, was a frail old woman.

"Mercy," she cried. "Don't kill me, Blacktooth."

"I'm not Blacktooth," said Gunner.

"Oh, no," cried the poor woman. "M-monsters! Ghostly monsters with faces cursed." She covered her eyes and sobbed.

"She's not very fierce for a cannibal," said Mozzy. "The poor thing is so skinny she could slide down a plug hole."

"We'll get no sense out of her," said Slicer. "She's petrified."

"She's old," said Mahoot, "and she needs help." He rushed to the old woman's side. "Don't worry," he said. "We're friendly." His voice had the right effect and the old woman looked up. She took in the sight of the three boys. Al smiled and held out his hand in friendship. Cautiously, the old woman reached out her bony hand and touched Mahoot.

"We're running away from Blacktooth too," Al told her. "He's after us."

The old woman searched the boys' eyes with hers. "I see you are telling the truth," she said. She shuddered as she looked at the other pirates. "But your friends are terrible to gaze upon."

"We need some help," said Captain Gunner, his voice honking through his swollen nose. "Is there somewhere safe from Blacktooth?"

The old woman stood up. "You promise you won't hurt us?"

"We promise," the pirates said in unison.

"Come with me, then."

They followed the old woman down a narrow track that wove, maze-like, through the jungle until they found themselves approaching a village of bamboo huts. An old man appeared at a doorway. He took one look at the dirty and frightening band of men and ran off.

"Stop!" called the old woman after him. "Come back! These men are running from Blacktooth. We must help them."

The old man hesitated. Gunner tried a friendly wave.

"They look worse than they are," said the woman. So the man returned and held out

his frail hand to Captain Gunner.

"I am the chief of this tribe," he said, calling the rest of the tribe to come out of their hiding places. The villagers stared suspiciously at the new arrivals.

The boys soon discovered there were only a few very thin men and women and some half-starved children in the cannibal village. The chief politely welcomed the crew, bowing low and humbly inviting them to sit down and dine.

A few fresh fish, a roast chicken and some vegetables foraged from the jungle were laid on banana leaf mats in front of Gunner and his crew. The hungry pirates tucked in to the food with gusto, but Al noticed that the cannibals weren't eating. He hoped they weren't just trying to fatten them up.

"Why aren't you eating?" Al asked a young man beside him.

"There is not enough for us," the young

man replied, watching hungrily as Captain Gunner chomped on a chicken drumstick. "Blacktooth has us beaten. We are hungry, but you are our first guests in many years. All we have is before you."

"You have nothing?" Jack asked, shocked by the young man's words.

"We have nothing," the man responded. "And our situation worsens by the day. Some of us went looking for fruit and vegetables last week, but they went too far from our village. We think Blacktooth has killed them or captured them to sell as slaves." He wiped away a tear. "My brother was one of them."

"So you're not cannibals?" Al asked.

"Goodness me, no," replied the chief, who overheard. "Many years ago a pirate came here. He killed many of us and he stole our gold. Vicious Victor, he called himself. Afterwards, we made the shrunken heads to frighten him in case he came back. They are our only protection. Then Blacktooth came and built his fort. He guards the only entrance to the island. We cannot escape or trade. Luckily, he thinks we will eat him, so he keeps away from our village."

"That's terrible," said Jack. He turned to

Captain Gunner. "Can we help them?"

"We can if you'll help us," Gunner said to the chief. "We have to keep Blacktooth away from us while we hunt for the treasure hidden on your island. If we find the treasure, we'll give you enough to see you right."

"But money and jewels are no use to

these people if they can't use it to trade with the outside world," Al pointed out.

Captain Gunner scratched his swollen nose and looked puzzled. "Yes, that is indeed a problem," he agreed.

Eaten by Cannibals

Gunner and the chief sat beside a warm fire that evening. The boys sat opposite. Gunner held the treasure map out so the chief could study it. "See, the treasure is marked by a Jolly Roger," Gunner said, pointing to a mark on the map. "But from the shrunken heads onwards the map is blank. Have you ever come across the cave that's mentioned on the map?"

The chief shook his head. "No, there are

many caves on the island. We could search, but large trees hide many of the caves and the paths are overgrown."

Captain Gunner sighed. "We need more clues," he despaired. "There are too many traps and Blacktooth's hunting for us. We can't just wander around." He waved the map in the air. "If only we could find the missing part of the map!"

The firelight glowed through the paper and Al noticed something strange about it. "Can I look at the map, please?" he asked Gunner. "I think there is a secret hidden on it."

Gunner passed the map over and Al took it closer to the fire. It was blank, yet when he had seen it through the flames, he was sure he'd seen something more. He took the paper closer and closer to the flickering firelight.

"Hey!" yelled Gunner. "Be careful or you'll burn it!"

But Al kept holding the map against the heat until the paper turned brown. To his delight the map began to change. A pathway and several Jolly Roger flag markers mysteriously appeared. There was one flag beside a sharp rock, another near a rounded hill, another beside a waterfall and finally one near a cliff on a hill.

"That's magic!" cried Mahoot.

"No," Al said to him, "that's lemon juice. It's a way of writing secret words. You write them with lemon juice and you can only see them by heating the paper." He handed the map back to Gunner, smiling. "I think we can find that treasure now."

Captain Gunner grinned back. "Now, how do we get Blacktooth to go away so we can start our hunt?"

"I have another idea," said Al. "But before I tell you, how are we going to destroy Blacktooth's grip on the island?"

"We have to distract him, then capture his fort," said Gunner. "If he's busy in the jungle, we can head to his fort and take it over while it's empty."

"I think we can do both things at once," said Al. He leant over and, in a low voice, explained his plan to Gunner and the chief.

The chief broke out in a broad smile and Captain Gunner slapped his knees with joy. "Al, you're a clever one," he cried. He turned to his crew and pointed to Mahoot, Slicer and two other pirates. "I want you four to stay here. Al will tell you what he wants you to do, then he and the rest of the crew are coming with me to the fort."

Before Al, Jack, Gunner and the crew left the village, each pirate gave his hat to the village women. Then, gathering a big ball of muddy clay, each of them pushed his face into the mud, leaving their imprint.

Afterwards, Mahoot and the remaining

pirates worked all night with the villagers, who arrived with large pots of sticky white sap. After pouring the sap into the clay prints they put them into a big pot, letting them heat slowly over a fire. Then the villagers took the prints out of the pots and pulled the sticky sap away, which was now firm and skin-like. They collected coconuts, one for each man, and wrapped the rubbery skin around the coconuts. Finally, they

painted them and added hair and hats.

Some of the villagers went out into the jungle to search for Blacktooth. Just before daylight they returned with the news that the pirate and his crew were camped nearby.

Captain Blacktooth awoke to the sound of warlike drumbeats. "The cannibals are aroused," whispered one of his men fearfully. "They know we're here."

"It's not uss they've sseen," said Blacktooth, "or we'd have a ssspear through our throatsss by now. They've probably come upon Gunner and his scabby crew."

As the words left his mouth, he heard a mighty howl of terror, the clashing of swords and the desperate shouts of men fighting for their lives.

"The cannibals have them," said Pigface, laughing wickedly. "Couldn't happen to a nicer bunch..." A blood-curdling death scream and a savage shriek of victory drowned Pigface's words.

"Ssomeone's just bitten the dusst," said Blacktooth. "Sstay quiet! We don't want to be found too."

The fight in the distance went on for an hour or more. Then one last piteous voice cried, "Don't kill me! I'm only a cabin boy! They're all dead. I'm only little, you don't need to eat me too!"

Blacktooth smiled at the tragic plea. "If that elephant-loving

kid'ss the only one left, then they're all dead," he gloated. Another chilling death scream followed, making Blacktooth's smile grow wider and wider until he revealed his one remaining black tooth.

Then there was silence.

"We sstay low for an hour or sso," ordered Blacktooth. "I think the cannibalss have done our work for uss. No one'ss left of *The Booty*'ss crew. We'll wait till we think the cannibalss are feassting at their camp. Then it'll be ssafe to move."

Blacktooth's men waited patiently until they heard the cannibal drums beating again, but this time it was the happy beat of a celebration. A wisp of smoke appeared over the tops of the trees.

"I guess that's them being cooked," said Flash, Captain Blacktooth's cabin boy. "If the cannibals are busy eating," he added nervously, "we could get to the fort now, before it's too late."

Blacktooth agreed with a nod of his head. The pirates stood up and crept down the path back towards the Shrunken Head Jungle. Imagine their terror when they looked up and saw the fresh heads of Gunner and his crew, still wearing their hats, glaring down upon them from high up in the trees.

"They must have died a horrible death," whispered Pigface, shuddering in revulsion as he stared at the terrible swellings on his enemies" faces. "Look how badly they've been beaten."

Looking away, Blacktooth pushed the man in front of him. "Hurry, let'ss get back to *The Revenge* fasst."

Back on board *The Revenge*, Blacktooth eyed the empty *Booty* riding at anchor. "Lower a boat and secure *The Booty*," he ordered. "We'll take her home – she'll

make a bit on the market."

But before his orders could be carried out, Flash pointed to the south. "Look, smoke!" he yelled. "Something big is on fire."

"That smoke's from our fort!" cried Pigface. "Who left the stove on?"

"What if our cannibal prisoners have escaped?" said Flash.

"Ssludgy sskullss!" Blacktooth cursed. "Our fort'ss on fire! Forget *The Booty*! Sset ssail sstraightaway!"

The Fall of Blacktooth's Fort

Blacktooth's wooden fort stood on a cliff, overlooking the ocean. The solid ramparts towered ten metres above the ground and the only way in was through a huge, rough-hewn doorway that faced a steep track leading down to the ocean. Gunner's crew heaved at the door. It was locked tight and unbelievably strong.

"We could burn down the walls and get inside that way," suggested Slicer.

"What if there are captives trapped inside and the fire spreads?" said Mozzy. "We have to get inside first."

"Great idea," said Gunner. "But have you got the key?"

"If I were Blacktooth," said Al, "I would hide it somewhere. I wouldn't take it to sea in case it dropped overboard or the ship sank. I'd hide it nearby."

"I reckon you're right," Captain Gunner said, squinting at the sky. "Sun's come up and we can't waste time. Everyone spread out. Turn over the rocks. Look in trees."

The crew leapt to his command. Al and Jack went down the steep path towards the ocean. "If I'd just come off a ship, I wouldn't want to walk too far to find a key," Al said. "So let's begin close to the door."

"Let's look for a stone that looks quite clean," suggested Jack, "because if it hides the key it wouldn't collect much dirt - it would be picked up a lot."

As they began turning stones, a loud "meow" interrupted them. Al looked around. "Snakeboot!" he called. The cat replied with another loud cry. He sat just above the track in the sun with his purple eyes half-closed, looking happy and relaxed. Jack leapt up the bank and picked him up. "Hey, Al, Snakeboot's sitting on a rock with a Jolly Roger carved on it," he said.

"You'd never see it from the track," said Al as he jumped up beside Jack. "Now, is there a flat rock nearby?" Then the boys noticed a smooth white rock. They rolled it over and underneath was a large brass key. "Got it!" they cried.

Within minutes *The Booty*'s crew were inside the fort. The pirates spread out, exploring and opening doors.

"We might find Blacktooth's treasure," said Mozzy, rubbing his hands with glee.

"I wonder if the missing people from the village are here?" said Jack.

"You're right," said Al. "Let's search for them. Look for a door that's locked from the outside or barricaded in some way. A prison that would be easy to enter, but impossible to escape."

At one end of the fort the boys found a barred and locked door. A key hung from a hook close by. Unsure of what they might find, the boys lifted the bar and unlocked the door. Inside sat several desperate-looking people. "Captain Gunner!" Jack called out. "We've found the missing hunting party."

As soon as the villagers were released, Captain Gunner took them to Blacktooth's kitchen. He handed them bags of flour, sugar, rice and salt. "I think you should go home now," he said. "Your families are

hungry, and they'll be glad to see you. We're gunner secure the fort so Blacktooth'll never trouble you again."

With a great deal of smiling and laughter, the villagers left the pirate fort carrying their riches.

Captain Gunner wanted to find Blacktooth's weapons so his men would be well armed if it came to a fight with their bitter enemy. He strode over to a large storeroom beneath the lookout tower.

Opening the door to a huge pitch-black room with no windows, Gunner fumbled around, found a lantern, lit it and placed it on a box for light. Al and Jack followed the captain inside.

Barrels of gunpowder, cannonballs, weapons of all sorts, spare ropes and sails were piled on top of each other. Snakeboot, curious as ever, ran into the room and began to explore. When Al moved a box, a large rat jumped out, startling him.

Snakeboot chased it. The rat dodged and the cat jumped, missing it. The rat squealed and leapt onto the box with the lantern. Snakeboot flew after it, knocking the lantern over. With a splintering of glass the lantern crashed to the ground. Its oily flames caught hold of dusty sailcloth and flared.

With barrels of gunpowder all around them, Captain Gunner wasted no time. He grabbed the cat and, shielding it with one arm, hooked the boys by their frockcoat collars and pulled them out of the room. "Run, boys!" he yelled. "Run for your lives!"

Al and Jack needed no further warning and raced away from the storeroom. "She's gunner blow!" cried Captain Gunner. "Get out! Abandon ship!"

The crew stopped what they were doing and, seeing flames, took to their heels and bolted out of the fort. As they passed through the front gate a massive explosion threw them all to the ground and blasted the building apart. Wood and metal rained down on them, then a roaring fire broke out and the flames leapt high into the air.

Al and Jack picked themselves up and moved back from the heat and billowing smoke.

"Well," said Captain Gunner, holding the cat out for everyone to see. "I was gunner burn the fort down, but Snakeboot did it for me!"

Sapphires and Rubies

Cheers greeted Gunner and his crew when they returned to the village. The villagers brought out drums, whistles and stringed instruments and a great celebration began. Everyone sang and danced. The pirates skipped a jig and showed Al and Jack how to do the hornpipe, which the boys thought was a very odd dance indeed.

Jack made everyone laugh by showing them his breakdance moves. "And now I'll

do a moonwalk," he told them.

"Moonwalk is a bit of a silly name for a dance," said Mahoot.

"People have been to the moon," Al tried to explain, "and they have walked on it. There's no gravity, you see, so your arms and legs go all slow and strange."

"You're so funny!" laughed Slicer. "The moon is a little ball in the sky. If a man could stand on it, well, you would see him."

"You boys have the silliest ideas," added Mozzy.

"Do the dance again, though," laughed Mahoot. "It's so funny. Moonwalk! Ha, ha!" When Jack danced some more, Mahoot laughed till tears ran down his face.

The following day, fed and relaxed, the pirate crew set off with the treasure map. This time the map was easy to follow and the pirates made good progress.

"Two thousand paces east and sight a sharp rock at ten o'clock," said Gunner. They found the first Jolly Roger easily, as well as the other markers.

Soon they reached a rock overhang at the base of a large hill. "It should be in there," said Gunner, "but be careful as you go. Vicious Victor was always one for mantraps."

Carefully, they walked forward. Al studied his feet, and it was only luck that his eye caught a rope almost buried by fallen leaves. "Stop!" he shouted.

The men moved back and Captain Gunner inspected the snare. "We should spring it so no one is hurt in the future," he said. He undid the sash around his chest and dropped to the ground. Carefully he tied the sash to the hidden rope. "All of you lie down, too," he ordered. When everyone was safe, he pulled the rope. Whhhizzz. About ten large spears shot over their heads and embedded themselves in the trees.

"Wow!" said Jack. "That was close."

Once again the pirates moved forward cautiously until they entered the cavern. "There's treasure here for sure," said Gunner, "because Victor has left his sign."

Sitting at the back of the cave was a headless dead man. His arms rested across his chest and his skull sat on his knees. Two crossed swords lay in the dirt in front of the corpse. Gunner ignored the dead pirate and studied the map. "X marks the spot," he said. "This is where we dig."

Jack picked up one of the swords. The words 'The property of Vicious Victor, scourge of the Dragon Blood Islands' were scratched into the blade. He tucked the sword into his belt. "Might need this, even if it is famous," he thought to himself.

The Booty's crew hacked at the earth with their swords and sabres, and finally uncovered a large chest. After much heaving, they dragged it out of its resting place.

As Gunner went to lift the lid he noticed some faded writing. "It says, 'This is the property of Prince Alleric, of the Dragon

Blood Sabre.' And underneath someone has put all these numbers," said Gunner. "Is it some sort of secret code?" He looked at Al. "Can you read it? We shouldn't open the lid in case there's another trap."

Al studied the code. He looked for the most frequently used numbers to see if there was a pattern.

Dragon Blood Pirates
www.dragonbloodpirates.co.uk
Q: What lies at the bottom of the ocean and twitches?
A: A nervous wreck!
ORCHARD BOOKS
Not suitable for children under 36 months due to small parts
© Orchard Books 2010

25,15,21 1,18,5 3,21,18,19,5,4 9,6
25,15,21 20,1,11,5 20,8,9,19 6,15,18
25,15,21,18,19,5,12,6. 18,15,2,2,5,4
25,15,21 23,9,12,12 2,5 9,6 25,15,21
4,15,14,'20 7,9,22,5 9,20 1,23,1,25.

"It's a pretty easy code," Al said after a minute or two. "Each number stands for a letter of the alphabet. It says, 'You are cursed if you take this for yourself. Robbed you will be if you don't give it away.'"

"Vicious Victor would never have left that message," said Gunner. "Who has dug up the chest and put that on it?"

"This is really weird," agreed Al. "Why not come and take the treasure and do some good yourself?"

"Maybe it was the dead man guarding the chest as a dead man's curse can never be broken," said Slicer. "We must give the treasure away."

"We're gunner," said Gunner. "We're gunner help the people here who've had it so hard." Gunner began to lift the lid of the treasure chest.

"It's easier to give away something you've never seen," warned Al. "Perhaps we shouldn't open it, but take it down to the village and give it away immediately."

Gunner and the pirates stared at Al in horror. "Not look?" cried Mozzy. "Not even one peep at what we came so far to find?"

"Never," agreed Gunner. "We're gunner look." He lifted the lid defiantly.

"Sapphires!" cried Slicer.

"There's gold and emeralds, diamonds and pearls!" Captain Gunner lifted out a glittering red stone for all to see. "And mighty rubies!" he cried.

"We can't give it all to the natives," argued Mozzy. "We could take a few bags for ourselves and give the rest away. There's enough here for all of us."

Greed glittered in the pirates' eyes as brightly as the treasure in the chest. Captain Gunner nodded in agreement. "Everyone fill your pockets," he said. "No one will ever know, and the natives will be as happy as can be with all the rest."

"What about the curse?" asked Jack. But the pirates ignored him, grabbing fistfuls of jewels and put them in their pockets. "Now hoist the trunk and off we'll go," said Gunner.

Back at the village, the pirates gave the almost-full treasure trunk to the chief. "There's enough here to set you right forever," Gunner said as he watched the chief lift the lid.

The tribespeople couldn't believe their eyes at their sudden wealth. "We cannot take all of this," said the chief. "You have been so kind and good to us. Captain Gunner, you must take some for yourselves."

"If you insist," said Captain Gunner, and a greedy sparkle lit his eyes once again. He picked up an empty flour bag lying on the ground and tossed several sapphires and rubies into it.

"That's just terrible," Al whispered.

"Greedy pig," agreed Jack.

"I heard that!" said Captain Gunner.

"We're pirates, not charity workers. We earned this." He held his hand out to the chief. "Well, we must be off. We'd better sail while the breeze holds and before Blacktooth recovers and comes after *The Booty*."

The pirates farewelled the villagers and set off back to their ship. Whistling as they walked, there was a happy spring to their step. "That treasure will do them no good,

I'm sure of it," Al said to Jack. "It was stolen from Prince Alleric."

Jack was deep in thought. "Has it ever occurred to you," he said, "that your surname is an anagram of sabre?"

Al raised an eyebrow in surprise. "No," he said, "it hadn't! I'd love to know where the Dragon Blood Sabre is... Come to think of it, I'd also like to know where Snakeboot has got to." Al looked around. "We can't leave him here."

"There he is," said Jack, pointing. "He's going into the hollow tree where we found the old woman." The boys ran over towards the cat and climbed inside the tree trunk. "O-oh," said Jack as he felt his arms and legs tingle. "I think we're going home again."

Hally's Plea

Jack and Al quickly changed out of their pirate clothes, went downstairs and sat on the couch. They made themselves comfortable and turned on the TV.

"You know," said Al, "I think we

should go back to the Dragon Blood Islands as soon as possible. I want to find the sabre. Imagine what we could do with it."

Suddenly the front door flew open and Hally, Al's sister, ran into the room. Tears stained her face.

"What's up with you, Hally?" asked Al.

"The girls are teasing me," said Hally. "They say I don't look like a popstar because I've got curly hair!" She plonked herself down beside her brother and began to cry.

"The pirates say you look just like a princess," soothed Al, trying to cheer her up. Hally sobbed and wiped her nose with the back of her hand.

Jack giggled. "But when you do that you look like Snotty Nell."

Hally wiped her nose again. "Can I play with you?" she asked.

"Pirates?" asked Al. "You didn't like it last time you were with us."

Hally looked a little worried. "It was pretty scary," she agreed, "but I want to be Princess Halimeda and wear my old-fashioned dress."

"But I don't think there's a place on pirate ships for a princess," argued Al. "We might be at sea in a storm and you'd get sick. It's better if you stay here. What if you threw up all over your dress? We wouldn't clean you up."

"I want to go!" Hally squealed. "And I'll cry and cry if you don't let me."

Jack looked at Al in disgust. Al rolled his eyes, exasperated. "You're being very annoying now," he said.

"I'll be good if you take me. Just one more time," Hally begged.

"We'll think about it, okay?" said Jack.

"Okay," sniffed Hally. She jumped up, happy again. "I'm off to my room to read."

When she left, Jack as Al, "We're not going to take her, are we? She's a bit of a pain."

Al shook his head. "Come over really early tomorrow and we'll leave without her. We can be back before she knows we're gone. Then we'll say we're playing football. She hates football."

Clues to the Puzzles

On page 81, Al and his friends come across a numerical code, where each number stands for a letter of the alphabet.

Here is a similar code for you to decipher:

23,8,1,20 4,15 25,15,21 3,1,12,12
1 8,1,16,16,25 16,9,18,1,20,5?
10,15,12,12,25 18,15,7,5,18!

If you are in doubt as to how Al cracked the code or need help solving the one above, visit www.dragonbloodpirates.co.uk

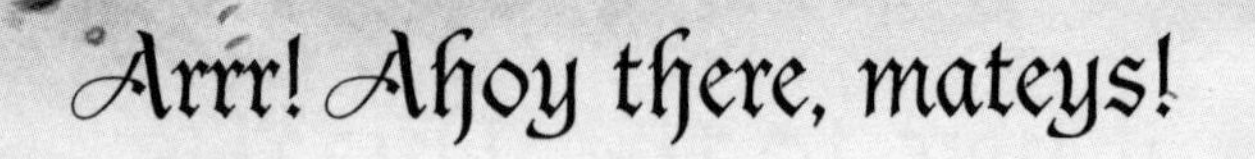

Hoist the sails and drop the anchor: ye have some treasure to find!

One swashbucklin' reader will win a haul of booty, including an Xbox console and games and an iTunes voucher, and twelve runners up will win a Dragon Blood Pirates booty bag.

For a chance to win, ye must dare to unearth the treasure using the Dragon Blood Islands map from *Death Diamond* (also available to download at www.dragonbloodpirates.co.uk), and the six big pirate stickers that are inserted in every book.

Each of the six Dragon Blood Pirates books contains a clue revealing an island protected by a dastardly pirate, and a sticker of the pirate to place on your map. When ye have solved the six clues, and have placed the six stickers, there will remain only one island, where the pirate booty be.

To win, enter online at
www.dragonbloodpirates.co.uk

Or send your name, address and the name of the island where the treasure lies to:

Dragon Blood Pirates Treasure Hunt
338 Euston Road, London NW1 3BH

Best o'luck, me hearties!

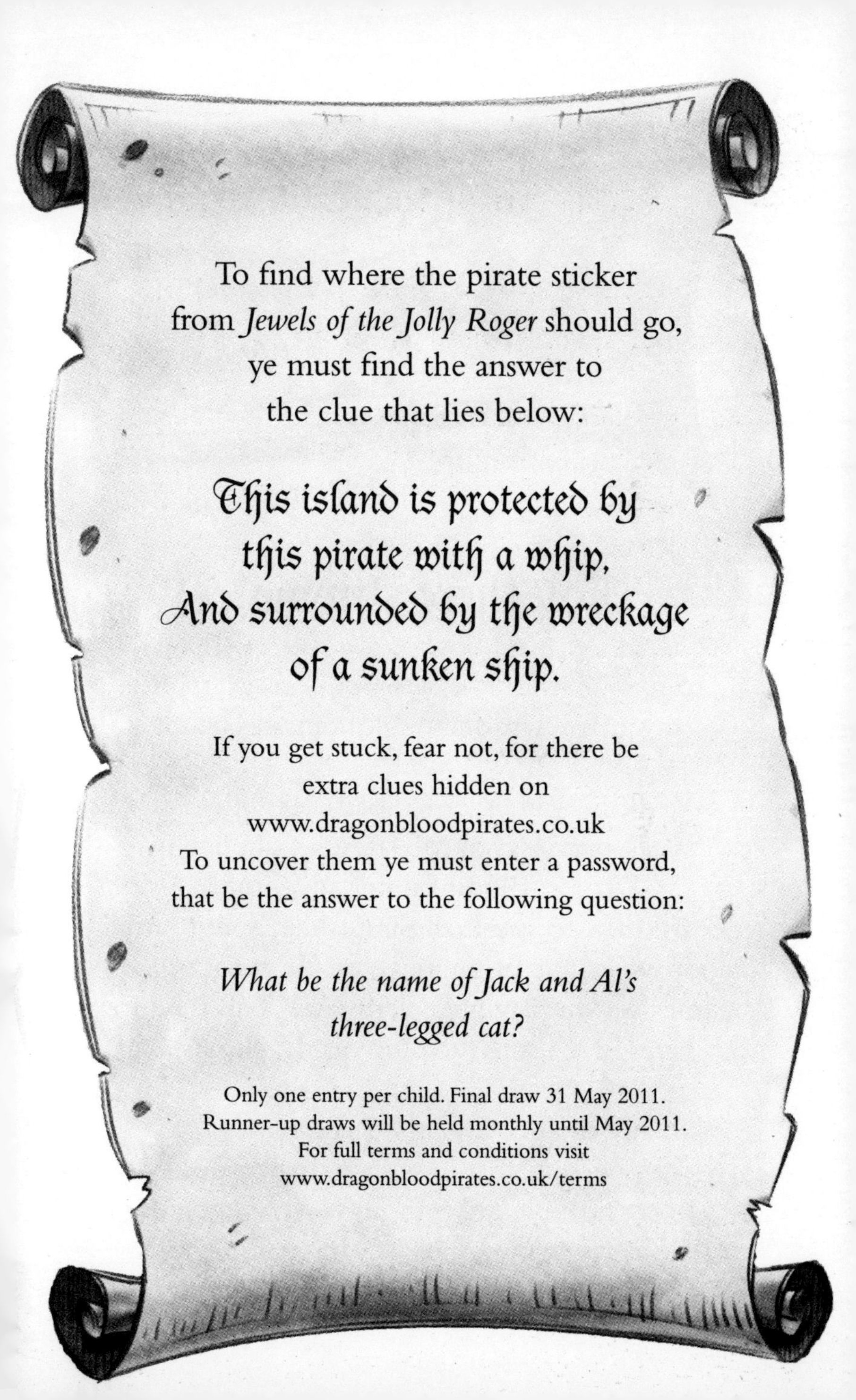
To find where the pirate sticker
from *Jewels of the Jolly Roger* should go,
ye must find the answer to
the clue that lies below:
This island is protected by
this pirate with a whip,
And surrounded by the wreckage
of a sunken ship.
If you get stuck, fear not, for there be
extra clues hidden on
www.dragonbloodpirates.co.uk
To uncover them ye must enter a password,
that be the answer to the following question:
What be the name of Jack and Al's
three-legged cat?
Only one entry per child. Final draw 31 May 2011.
Runner-up draws will be held monthly until May 2011.
For full terms and conditions visit
www.dragonbloodpirates.co.uk/terms

Ahoy there shipmates!

To reel in amazin' pirate booty, steer smartly towards www.dragonbloodpirates.co.uk

Ye'll find games, downloads, activities and sneak previews of the latest swashbucklin' Dragon Blood Pirates adventures. Learn how to speak all pirate-like, how to find out what type of pirate ye be, an' what pirate games ye can play with yer mates! This treasure trove is a sure feast fer yer deadlights!

Only the bravest an' heartiest amon' ye can become a true scurvy dog, so don't ye miss a thing and sign up to yer newsletter at www.dragonbloodpirates.co.uk!

Don't ye miss book five in the

Dragon Blood Pirates

series!

Turn the page and shiver yer timbers
with a slice of the next high-seas adventure...

Kidnapped

Alleric Breas looked around in surprise. He was in a small room filled with barrels and boxes. There were no windows, but a dim light came through large cracks in the door. His sister, Hally, squeezed his hand tightly in apprehension.

Just then Jack Seabrook, Al's best friend, began to appear. He shimmered, mist-like, then solidified. In his arms was their three-legged, purple-eyed pirate cat, Snakeboot.

They heard wind roaring in the rigging and waves crashing against a wooden hull, followed by the strong smell of seawater and oilcloth.

"Do you think we're in the cabin of a ship sailing through the Dragon Blood Islands?" Jack asked.

Al glanced around. "It's too small for a cabin. By the look of all the boxes here, I'd say we're in some sort of storeroom."

"I'll try the door," said Jack. "I'll peek out and see where we've landed this time."

The trio had just arrived from number five Drake Drive, in the twenty-first century. Only minutes before, the boys had gone into Al's attic, where they'd found Hally waiting for them, dressed in her princess clothes, ready to visit the Dragon Blood Islands. The boys then changed into their sea-going pirate clothes, and Jack belted on the pirate sword he'd found on Cannibal Island. Al took Hally's hand and unlocked their old sea trunk. He put the key in his pocket, opened the lid, and together they stepped inside.

Jack picked up Snakeboot and followed. Within seconds they had vanished from the attic.

The boys had hoped to return to Cannibal Island, where they'd previously left Captain Gunner and his pirate crew, but instead they found themselves inside the storeroom of a sailing ship.

The ship tacked suddenly and Hally lost her balance and fell over. Jack clutched at the door and gave it a push. "Door's locked," he said.

Al lifted the lid of a barrel and checked inside. "It's gunpowder," he said.

"I hope this is the storeroom on *The Booty*," said Jack.

"We could see if it's Captain Gunner's ship by looking for the sapphires and rubies he stole from those poor tribes people on Cannibal Island," suggested Al.

"Does Captain Gunner really have

sapphires and rubies?" asked Hally, brightening at the mention of jewels.

"Loads of them," replied Jack, "and if this is *The Booty*'s storeroom, then they might be in here."

"We should look around anyway," said Al. "It'll give us a clue as to what ship we've landed in. Luckily we didn't land on a rock with that horrible shark, Greeny Joe, trying to eat us."

"Shark?" cried Hally. "You never told me about any shark."

"He's huge," said Jack, enjoying Hally's look of fear, "with massive teeth. Greeny Joe's covered in green mould, so he glows in the dark. He chewed up Snotty Nell."

"Greeny Joe's got a real thing for Snotty," added Al. "She smells like a big Christmas pudding and Greeny Joe follows her everywhere trying to get another bite."

Hally shivered as she remembered

the horrible pirate who'd kidnapped the elephants on Sabre Island. "Snotty's a nasty old grouch," she said, "but it must be awful to have a shark following you around all the time, trying to eat you." She took a small step towards a cupboard and opened it. A carved wooden chest sitting high up on a shelf caught her eye. "What do you think's in *that*?" she said, standing on tiptoes, but she was too small to reach. "I can't get it."

Al reached up and pulled at the chest. "It's heavy," he grunted as he brought it down. When he opened the lid Hally gasped in surprise as glittering blue and red gems glowed in the darkened room.

"So many!" she cried. "Are they real?"

"Yes, they are," said Jack, inspecting the treasure. "So now we've worked out we're on Gunner's ship, how will we explain how we got here, and with Hally?"

Al shrugged. Captain Gunner would never believe they just sneaked on board and locked themselves in the ship's storeroom.

"Can I keep some of the jewels?" asked Hally, oblivious to the problem at hand. She fingered the gems and rolled a few of them in the palm of her hand.

"They're cursed," Jack told her.

Hally dropped the jewels immediately. "Are they?" she asked. "I don't believe you."

"I'm serious. A deadman's curse," said Jack. "If these jewels aren't used for good, someone will steal them."

"You have to give them away for a good cause," explained Al, "and although Captain Gunner gave away most of the jewels he found, he couldn't help himself and stole these."

As Al spoke, *The Booty* tacked again and the children were tossed to one side of the small room. The treasure chest tipped over, spilling the gems across the floor. They had just begun to pick them up when they heard a cannon being fired, followed by another hard tack.

"Oh, no, we're being attacked," cried Jack. "Get down low."

Al, Jack and Hally sat on the floor and waited anxiously as musket fire and yelling thundered around them. Shortly afterwards the grinding of wood on wood and a deafening crunch told them they had collided with another ship. They heard the sails billowing and flapping as *The Booty* was hauled into the breeze, followed by the screams and shouts of a sword fight. They listened in fear to the war cries of the boarding pirates.

"If the invaders win," said Al, "they'll head straight for this storeroom."

"I hope it's not Blacktooth," declared

Jack. "I don't think he'd be a happy man after having his fort blown up."

"Snotty's not too keen on us either," said Al, "but I'd rather it was her. She's got a child of her own so I doubt she'd kill us."

"Oh!" wailed Hally. "I only wanted to play princesses; I didn't want to get killed!"

Her words had barely left her mouth when the storeroom door burst open and Snotty Nell, waving a sabre, pushed her way into the room. Her one good eye flashed with the fire of battle. When it fell upon the pile of jewels it flashed with the fire of greed. "Who'd have thought old Gunner would have such riches?" she roared. "Sneaky old fool." When she saw the children she took a step back. She wiped a long green booger from her scarred nose. "And who'd think he'd have three children locked up in the storeroom?" She peered at Hally. "A girl!"

"A princess," said Hally. "Princess Halimeda."

Al's eyebrows shot up at Hally's words.

"A princess, are you?" snarled Snotty Nell. "Then that box of jewels would explain a lot. That must be your ransom payment." She turned on Al and Jack. "And you two rapscallions, you have robbed me of a diamond, and you owe me!" She took an angry step towards Jack and shook her sabre.

Jack reached for the sword in his belt. Quick as a viper, Snotty grabbed his hand, pulled the sword away and tossed it behind her, pushing Jack to the floor. Al jumped to his feet to defend his friend, but Snotty grasped his shirt collar with her free hand and shook him angrily.

"Leave my brother alone!" Hally cried, then burst into tears.

"Oh? A brother?" growled Snotty. She stared hard at Al. "So the truth comes out." She turned her attention back to Jack. "You must be a royal too, or you wouldn't be locked up in here with these two. It explains why Gunner had you two on board last time. He was waiting for his ransom payment." Finally she put her sabre in its scabbard. "Vampire!" she bellowed.

A huge pirate appeared and leered at the children, baring his sharp-pointed teeth.

"Tie this lot up," Snotty said. "Don't harm them, but you know how tricky these boys can be, so put them in sacks where they can't wriggle free. We'll take them on board our ship with their lovely treasure." She pointed to the jewels spilled across the room.

"And when you three are on board, we'll put you to work," sneered Vampire Zu as he bound Al's hands together. "It'll do rich little smarty-pants like you a bit of good to work hard for the likes of us."

Minutes later, Hally, Jack and Al were trussed like turkeys, covered with large flour bags and hoisted onto the backs of Snotty's pirates to be taken on board her ship, *The Tormentor.*

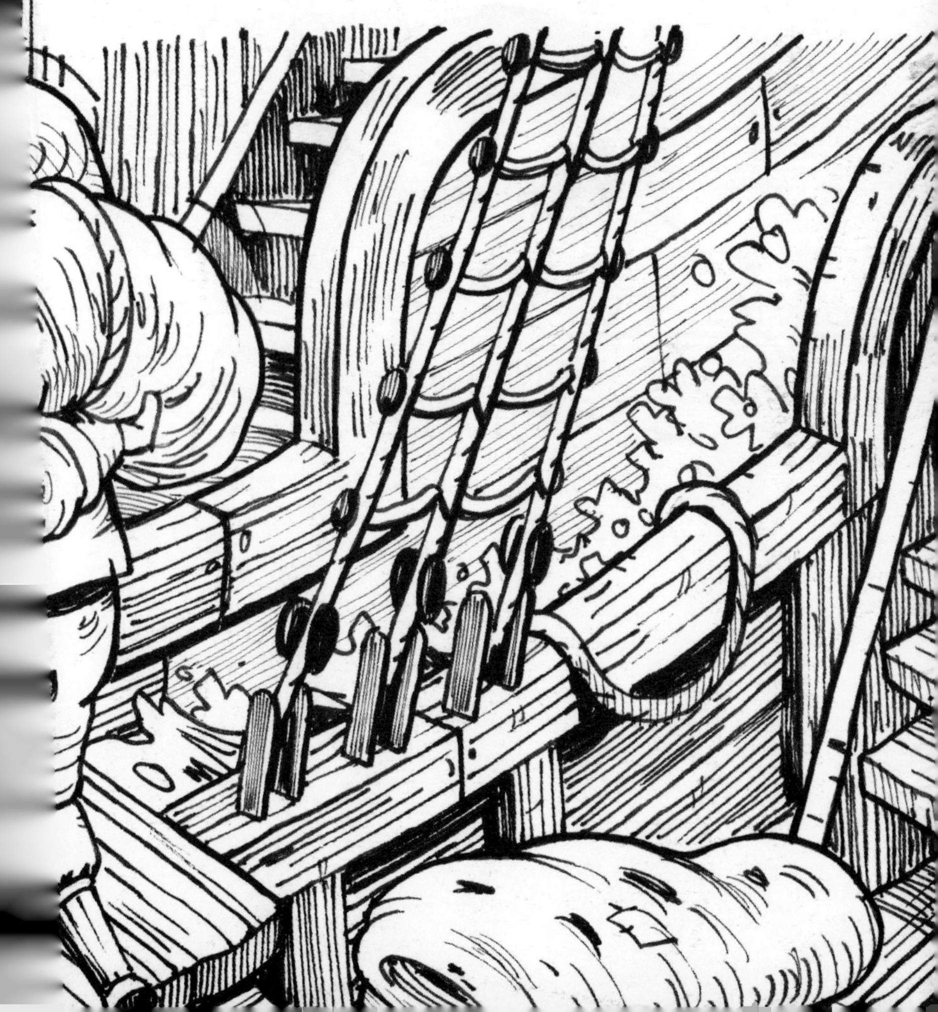